Tasha
the Tap Dance Fairy

by Daisy Meadows

SCHOLASTIC·INC.

New York   Toronto   London   Auckland   Sydney
Mexico City   New Delhi   Hong Kong   Buenos Aires

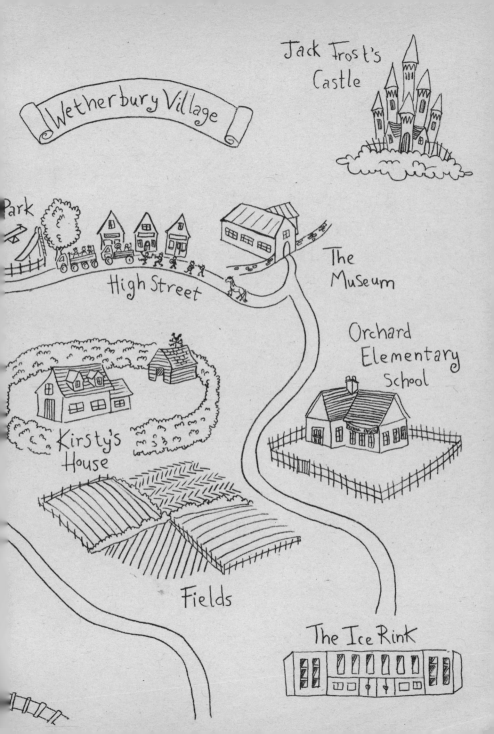

Hold tight to the ribbons, please.
You goblins may now feel a breeze.
I'm summoning a hurricane
To take the ribbons away again.

But, goblins, you'll be swept up too,
For I have work for you to do.
Guard each ribbon carefully,
By using your new power to freeze.

Contents

Tapping Trouble

"Wow," Kirsty Tate said, as she followed her mom through the door of Wetherbury College's main building and saw the crowds inside. "It's really busy in here!"

Her friend, Rachel Walker, who was staying with Kirsty over school break, nodded in agreement. She took off her

hat and stuffed it in her pocket as she looked around. "There's a pottery stand," she said, pointing it out. "Ooh, and look, they're decorating cakes over there!"

The girls had come with Kirsty's mom to the college Open House. This was a special event where people could find out

more about all the different courses the college offered. Since Mrs. Tate was taking a wood-carving class at the college, she'd volunteered to help out at the woodworking stand and answer any questions people might have. All around the hall there were display tables showing different skills taught at the college.

"There's the wood-carving stand,"
Mrs. Tate said, pointing it out to the
girls. "That's where I'll be all morning,
OK? But you can wander around
and look at everything else. There's
lots to see."

Rachel and Kirsty said good-bye and
headed off around the room.
They saw a man at the
pottery stand making a
vase on a potter's wheel.
Then they watched
as a makeup artist
transformed somebody
into a zombie at the special effects
makeup stand. It was amazing how
the thick white makeup and some fake
blood running down his chin made the
volunteer look completely different.

"Spooky," Kirsty whispered to Rachel with a shudder.

The makeup artist smiled at the girls. "You can create almost anything with the right makeup," she told them.

The "zombie" grinned. "It's pretty strange being turned into something else, though!" he said.

Rachel and Kirsty exchanged a smile. They knew all about being turned into something else. Thanks to their fairy friends, they'd been turned into fairies many times!

Only a few days earlier, Rachel and Kirsty had been plunged into another fairy adventure, this time helping the

Dance Fairies find their missing magic dance ribbons. So far, the girls had helped find three of the ribbons, but four others were still lost.

Just as Rachel was thinking about the Dance Fairies, Kirsty gave her a nudge.

"Look!" she said, pointing. "Tap dancers!"

Rachel turned to see. At the far end of the room, some girls in sparkly red tap shoes were practicing a routine. Rachel winced as one of them clumsily dropped her black cane on another dancer's foot. Almost immediately, the girl next to her tripped over it.

"There's the wood-carving stand," Mrs. Tate said, pointing it out to the girls. "That's where I'll be all morning, OK? But you can wander around and look at everything else. There's lots to see."

Rachel and Kirsty said good-bye and headed off around the room. They saw a man at the pottery stand making a vase on a potter's wheel. Then they watched as a makeup artist transformed somebody into a zombie at the special effects makeup stand. It was amazing how the thick white makeup and some fake blood running down his chin made the volunteer look completely different.

more about all the different courses the college offered. Since Mrs. Tate was taking a wood-carving class at the college, she'd volunteered to help out at the woodworking stand and answer any questions people might have. All around the hall there were display tables showing different skills taught at the college.

"There's the wood-carving stand," Mrs. Tate said, pointing it out to the girls. "That's where I'll be all morning, OK? But you can wander around and look at everything else. There's lots to see."

Rachel and Kirsty said good-bye and headed off around the room. They saw a man at the pottery stand making a vase on a potter's wheel. Then they watched as a makeup artist transformed somebody into a zombie at the special effects makeup stand. It was amazing how the thick white makeup and some fake blood running down his chin made the volunteer look completely different.

more about all the different courses the college offered. Since Mrs. Tate was taking a wood-carving class at the college, she'd volunteered to help out at the woodworking stand and answer any questions people might have. All around the hall there were display tables showing different skills taught at the college.

"Spooky," Kirsty whispered to Rachel with a shudder.

The makeup artist smiled at the girls. "You can create almost anything with the right makeup," she told them.

The "zombie" grinned. "It's pretty strange being turned into something else, though!" he said.

Rachel and Kirsty exchanged a smile. They knew all about being turned into something else. Thanks to their fairy friends, they'd been turned into fairies many times!

Only a few days earlier, Rachel and Kirsty had been plunged into another fairy adventure, this time helping the

Dance Fairies find their missing magic dance ribbons. So far, the girls had helped find three of the ribbons, but four others were still lost.

Just as Rachel was thinking about the Dance Fairies, Kirsty gave her a nudge.

"Look!" she said, pointing. "Tap dancers!"

Rachel turned to see. At the far end of the room, some girls in sparkly red tap shoes were practicing a routine. Rachel winced as one of them clumsily dropped her black cane on another dancer's foot. Almost immediately, the girl next to her tripped over it.

"Kirsty, did you see that?" she whispered. "Their dancing is falling apart already!"

Kirsty nodded. "And we both know why," she replied. "It's because Tasha the Tap Dance Fairy's ribbon is still missing!"

The girls had learned that the Dance Fairies used their ribbons to make sure that dancing, both in Fairyland and in the human world, went as smoothly as possible. Unfortunately, Jack Frost, a powerful and selfish fairy, had stolen the magic ribbons because he wanted his goblins to dance well at his parties.

When the fairy king and queen heard that the dance ribbons had been stolen,

they went straight to Jack Frost's ice
castle to get them back. But Jack Frost
saw them coming and cast a spell that
sent the ribbons into the human world,
with a goblin to guard each one.

Without their ribbons, the Dance
Fairies could not work their special
magic, and dancing everywhere was
going all wrong!

"Excuse me," came a voice
from behind the girls.
Rachel and Kirsty
turned to see a girl who
was about their age,
dressed in a leotard
like the other tap
dancers. "Have you seen
a pair of red tap shoes
and a black cane

anywhere?" she asked. "I won't be able to be part of the performance if I don't find them."

Kirsty shook her head. "Sorry, we haven't seen them," she replied.

The girl sighed. "Maybe they fell out of my bag in the parking lot when Mom dropped me off," she said.

"We'll go and look for them if you want," Rachel offered.

The girl's eyes brightened. "Oh, thank you," she said.

"I'll keep looking in here. I'm Ashleigh Hart, by the way."

"We're Kirsty and Rachel," Kirsty

replied, smiling, as Ashleigh waved and set off to search the rest of the room.

Kirsty and Rachel turned toward the entrance, but then stopped. They both heard a faint tapping sound. It was in perfect time to the tap dancers' music!

Tap-tap-tap-tappity-TAP! Tap-tap-tap-tappity-TAP!

Rachel looked over at the dancers

eagerly. Did this mean the magic tap dance ribbon was nearby, helping the dancers?

But the girls in the sparkly red tap shoes weren't actually dancing at all! *If they're not making the tapping sound, then who is?* Rachel wondered.

Tap-tap-tap-tappity-TAP! Tap-tap-tap-tappity-TAP!

"I think it's coming from over here," Kirsty said, walking toward the corner of the room.

Rachel followed. There was nothing there except a table with some leaflets on it, but the tapping definitely got louder as she and Kirsty approached. Curiously, the girls peeked under the table.

Tasha Turns Up

Rachel and Kirsty smiled to see a tiny
fairy, with her eyes closed, tap dancing
her way through an amazing routine
at super-speed. It was Tasha the Tap
Dance Fairy, of course! Nobody else
would have been able to dance so
beautifully while the tap dance ribbon
was missing. The fairy wore a stylish

black vest, black tights, tap shoes, and a
bright red skirt.

Kirsty gave a polite
cough and Tasha's
eyes flashed open.
"Oh, hello," she
said. "You caught
me! I just couldn't
resist dancing when
I heard the music."
"You're really good!" Rachel told her.
"I've never seen anyone tap dance so fast
before."

Tasha smiled.
"Thanks," she said.
"But it's a shame
the other tap
dancers are
having problems."

She sighed. "If only my tap dance ribbon were safely back on my wand where it belongs, then they wouldn't keep messing up!"

"Do you have any idea where your ribbon is?" Kirsty asked.

Tasha shook her head. "No," she said, "but I'm hoping it might be around here. Keep your eyes open for any goblins, girls!"

Rachel glanced around nervously. The goblins were Jack Frost's sneaky helpers, and she and Kirsty had managed to outwit them in the past. This time, though, Jack Frost had given the goblins a special

power. As long as a goblin had one of
the magic dance ribbons, he also had the
power to freeze people.

Kirsty and Rachel never liked meeting
the goblins, but now they felt even more
nervous than ever about running into
them. No one wants to be turned into an
ice cube!

"We were just about to go outside,"
Kirsty told Tasha. "One of the dancers
lost her shoes and cane, and we said we'd
help look for them."

Tasha looked thoughtful. "Lost her

shoes and cane?"
she repeated. "I
wonder if they're
really lost, or if
somebody is
borrowing them!"

"Like a goblin?" Rachel quickly suggested. "It's just the kind of thing a goblin would do!"

Tasha nodded, her eyes sparkling. "We'd better keep an eye out for goblins while we're looking for the shoes and cane," she said.

"Maybe we'll find your tap dance ribbon, too," Kirsty added hopefully. She pulled her coat pocket open. "Tasha, do you want to hide in here?"

Tasha fluttered out from under the table and dove into Kirsty's pocket. Her

glittery wings shimmered under the bright lights in the room. "Let's go!" she said eagerly.

As the girls walked outside, Kirsty pulled her scarf a little tighter around her neck, and Rachel put her hat back on.

The college parking lot was directly in front of them. "Let's walk around the outside," Kirsty suggested. "A pair

of red tap shoes shouldn't be too hard
to spot."

Kirsty and Rachel set off around the
parking lot, keeping an eye out for the
shoes and cane. They also thought they
might see a flash of green and a scurrying
goblin, but there was no sign of any
goblin mischief.

Suddenly, Tasha zoomed out of Kirsty's
pocket and twirled in the air, gazing out
around the parking lot. "I
can sense my ribbon!"
she declared. "I'm
sure it's somewhere
nearby."

By now, the girls
had done a full circle
of the parking lot and
were back outside the main

entrance. Rachel pointed to a
path leading around the
side of the college.
"How about looking
down there?" she
suggested.

Tasha
nodded.
"Good idea,"
she agreed.
"My ribbon
can't be far
away."

The three
friends walked
along the path.
They could hear the
tap dance music again

now, drifting out of an open
window.
"What was that?"
Tasha whispered
suddenly, hovering
in the air in front
of the girls.
Rachel and
Kirsty stopped
to listen. Kirsty
couldn't hear
anything
except the music
at first, but then
she heard a *tap-
tap-tap-tappity-tap*
in perfect time to
the rhythm.

"Those are definitely tap shoes!" Rachel said excitedly.

"And the tapping isn't coming from inside the building," Tasha added. "So it must be somebody else!"

"A goblin!" Kirsty and Rachel whispered at the same time.

The girls crept a little farther down the path and peeked cautiously around the next corner.

There, tapping away and humming to the music, was a goblin. On his feet were sparkly red tap shoes, and in his hand was a cane with Tasha's magic ribbon tied around it in a neat bow!

The Big Freeze

"Could he look any sillier?" Tasha muttered, holding back a laugh. "Come on," she said to Kirsty and Rachel. "Let's go and get my ribbon back!"

Kirsty, Rachel, and Tasha headed toward the goblin. He was far too busy dancing to notice them.

"I'll take my ribbon back now, please," Tasha said in a firm voice. The goblin jumped in surprise, then glared at her. "Can't you see I'm trying to dance?" he asked, annoyed. "I've lost my place now!" He rolled his eyes, then turned away and began tapping again.

"Well, that's too bad, because we've come to get the cane and shoes back, too," Kirsty told him. "They don't belong to you!"

The goblin stomped his foot and spun around. "You're ruining my

concentration!" he said. "How am I supposed to dance when I keep getting interrupted?"

"I've had enough!" Tasha snapped. "That's not your ribbon to be dancing with. Give it back!"

Just then, someone must have turned the volume up inside the building, because the music suddenly got louder. The goblin launched into another dance routine, twirling his cane in his hand as he tapped his feet.

He's good, Rachel thought, but she knew he was only dancing well because the

magic ribbon was close to him. The
dance ribbons were so powerful that they
could turn even the clumsiest dancer into
something special — just as long as he
was close enough to the ribbon.

The goblin seemed totally absorbed
in his dancing. His eyes were shut tight in
concentration as he tapped to the beat.
Gradually, he started tapping away from
the three friends and toward where the

music was drifting out of one of the
college's side doors.

"What's he doing?" Kirsty hissed. "If
he's not careful, someone will see him."

"I thought the goblins were supposed to
be hiding," Rachel said in a low voice.
"But he's not even trying."

Tasha grinned.
"That's because of
the ribbon," she
explained. "It
makes whoever has
it seek out music.
Whenever they hear a
tune, they have to dance.
Once they're dancing, they forget
about everything else!"

"Well, hopefully he'll forget about
us," Kirsty said, hurrying after the goblin.

"And then we can grab the ribbon while he's distracted."

The girls and Tasha followed the goblin right up to the door, but as he opened it, he noticed them and stopped.

"Are you still here?" he snapped. "Well, I'm warning you, don't come any closer or I'll freeze you!"

And with that, he slipped through the door and slammed it shut, right in the girls' faces!

"Hey!" cried Kirsty. She ran to the door and turned the handle, but it was stuck.

"Oh no!" she cried. "It won't open! We'll lose him!"

"It's OK, there's a window open up there," Tasha said, pointing. "I'll fly in and keep track of him."

Rachel and Kirsty pushed against the door as Tasha zipped in through the open window. "Do you think he locked it?" Rachel panted.

"I don't know. Whoa!" Kirsty cried as the door suddenly flew open.

She and Rachel tumbled inside just in time to see Tasha wave her wand. A stream of fairy magic whizzed through the air and over to the tap dance ribbon. Immediately, the ribbon began to untie itself from the cane in the goblin's hand. Rachel and Kirsty watched excitedly as Tasha rushed forward to grab it.

But at that same moment, the goblin spun around and touched the fairy with his gnarly green finger. "FREEZE!" he shouted. Tasha instantly turned to ice.

No longer able to fly, the little fairy dropped toward the ground like a tiny winged icicle.

Tasha's Tumble

As Tasha tumbled toward the floor, Rachel pulled off her hat and dove forward, holding it out in front of her. Fortunately, Rachel was just in time to softly catch Tasha in the hat before the frozen fairy hit the floor.

The goblin didn't seem to care. He just gave a mean cackle. "You pesky girls

will be next unless you leave me alone," he told them. "So stay away!"

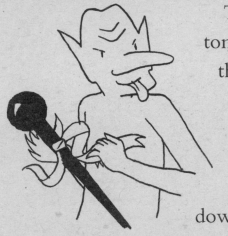

Then he stuck his tongue out, knotted the ribbon around his cane, and danced off down the hallway. Rachel looked down at Tasha, who was still frozen solid inside her hat. The

fairy's dark hair twinkled with frost, and her face had an icy blue tint to it.

"Oh, Tasha," Rachel said,

gently blowing on her to try to warm her
up. "Tasha, can you hear me?"

"How about holding her in your
hands?" Kirsty suggested. "They might
be warmer than the hat."

Rachel agreed and carefully scooped
the frozen fairy into her cupped
hand. But at that moment, the girls
heard footsteps coming down
the hallway. Before
Rachel could even
think about hiding
Tasha, a woman
appeared.

Kirsty gulped.
How were they
going to explain
a frozen fairy?

Before she could think of anything to say, the woman began to speak.

"What a pretty ice sculpture!" she cried, looking at Tasha. "So delicate! So lifelike! I didn't realize the college offered an ice-sculpting course."

Rachel could only manage a small smile in response. Both girls heaved a sigh of relief as the lady smiled back and went on her way.

"Phew," Rachel said. "That was close!"

Kirsty was about to reply when a tiny, fairy-sized sneeze came from Tasha. Both girls looked down hopefully and

smiled as Tasha opened her eyes.
Shivering, she stood up on Rachel's hand
and rubbed her arms.

"Tasha! Are you all
right?" Kirsty asked
anxiously.

Tasha sneezed
three more times,
flapped her wings
tentatively, and then
smiled. "I'm fine," she said.
"Luckily, the goblins' freezing power isn't
strong enough to freeze anyone for long.
The magic wears off quickly. And now
I'm more determined than ever to get my
tap dance ribbon back!"

Rachel nodded. "Come on," she said.
"Let's find that goblin!"

Tasha flew back into Kirsty's pocket

and the girls headed down the hallway, in the same direction that the goblin had gone. On their way, they caught a brief glimpse of Ashleigh in one of the classrooms, still hunting for her missing things.

"I hope she doesn't see you-know-who wearing her shoes," Kirsty muttered to Rachel as they went past.

They reached the main room, where the music was still playing. Kirsty looked over to where the tap dancers had been practicing and gasped in amazement. She couldn't believe who was dancing along with them. It was the goblin!

40

"Look at him!" Kirsty squealed, shocked to see him in such a busy, public place. "I can't believe nobody else has noticed him!"

Rachel stared hard. The goblin was *very* visible, tap dancing right in front of the speakers. "Oh, and look," she said, noticing something else. "The dancers around him are doing much better now. It must be because they're near the magic ribbon!"

The girls edged closer, not sure what to do. They wanted to grab the ribbon, but they didn't want to draw any more attention to the goblin.

"Look at that little green guy!" they heard a man say just then. "What a wonderful dancer!"

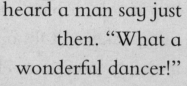

"He must have had his makeup done at the special effects stand," the man's friend replied. "I guess he's supposed to be some kind of goblin?"

"He does look kind of weird, with those big rubbery ears," another person commented. "They can do amazing things with makeup these days!"

Rachel had to clap her hand over her mouth to stop herself from giggling. Kirsty had to stifle a laugh, too.

"We've got to get him out of here," Tasha said. "It's fine as long as people think he's in costume, but what happens if someone realizes that he really is a goblin?"

Kirsty nodded, looking serious again. "That would be a disaster," she agreed. "And what if Ashleigh comes back and sees him dancing with her tap shoes and cane?"

"I don't know." Rachel sighed, looking anxious. "He's desperate to be near the music. He's as close as he can get to the speakers! How are we going to draw him away?"

Kirsty thought hard. The goblin was looking very pleased with himself. He was obviously enjoying his performance, and was even showing off to the other dancers! All his bragging gave her an idea.

"What if we challenge him to take part in a dance competition with you,

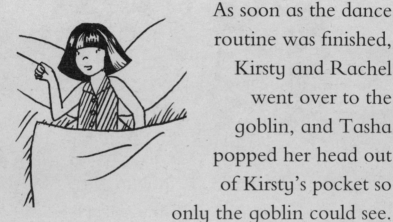

Tasha?" she suggested. "I bet he won't be able to resist trying to prove that he's the better tap dancer!"

Tasha grinned. "That sounds like an excellent plan!" she agreed.

As soon as the dance routine was finished, Kirsty and Rachel went over to the goblin, and Tasha popped her head out of Kirsty's pocket so only the goblin could see.

"Hey!" she called to the goblin. "You know, you're not *bad* at tap dancing, but you'll never be as good as me."

The goblin looked annoyed. "*Not bad?*" he spluttered. "I'm the best tap dancer in the world!"

46

Tasha laughed. "No way," she replied. "I'm the Tap Dance Fairy. I'm obviously the best!"

The goblin stopped dancing and stamped his foot. "No, *I* am!" he snapped.

Kirsty interrupted. "Why don't you two have a competition to settle it?" she suggested.

"Yes, if you're as good as you think you are, you should be able to follow Tasha's steps," Rachel told the goblin. "Or are you worried she'll be better than you?"

"No way!" The goblin snorted. "Just you watch. I'll do it, and I'll win!"

Kirsty smiled. "Oh, and there's one

more thing," she added. "If you're better than Tasha, we'll stop bothering you about the tap dance ribbon and you can keep it. But if you lose, you have to give it back."

The goblin hesitated, looking suspiciously from Tasha to Kirsty.

"Are you worried I'll win?" Tasha teased.

The goblin snorted. "As if!" he scoffed. "Of course you won't win. Let's go!"

Rachel smiled. "Let's find an empty classroom," she suggested. "Then we'll have more space for dancing."

The girls, the goblin, and Tasha all left the hall and found an empty room close

by, where they could still hear the tap
dance music.

Tasha hopped onto a desk. "Ready?"
she asked the goblin. He nodded. "Then
watch!"

She launched into a routine, tapping
her tiny fairy heels and toes on the
desktop, and finishing with a flourish of
her cane.

"Easy," the goblin said with a sneer.

He then copied her steps
perfectly.

"OK," Tasha said.
"Let's try another
one." She tapped
out a much more
complicated
routine.

This time the
goblin simply
shrugged. "No
problem," he
said, and copied
the routine
perfectly once
again. "Is that the
best you can do?" He
smirked.

Tasha raised an eyebrow.

"I'll show you the best I can
do," she responded. And,
with that, she threw
herself into a third
routine, her shoes
tapping like crazy
on the desktop,
her cane a blur as
she twirled and
twisted it in front
of her.

The goblin's
mouth fell open
as she finished.
"Ta-da!" Tasha
cried, twirling her
cane on one finger.
The goblin gulped.

"Ready when you are," Rachel
prompted.

The goblin squinted his eyes at her and
began tapping. Kirsty could tell that he
was trying his best, and he didn't look all
that bad, but the routine was just too
tricky for him. He tripped over his own
feet after a few moments.

Tasha smiled. "I
win," she said,
stretching out
a hand for the
ribbon.

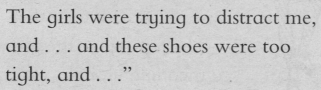

The goblin
shook his head,
panting. "No," he
argued. "That wasn't fair.
The girls were trying to distract me,
and . . . and these shoes were too
tight, and . . ."

Rachel was outraged to hear so many
excuses. "Tasha won the ribbon, fair and
square!" she said.

Tasha gave Rachel and Kirsty a secret
wink. "All right," she told the goblin.
"I'll give you one last chance. I bet you
can't do this!"

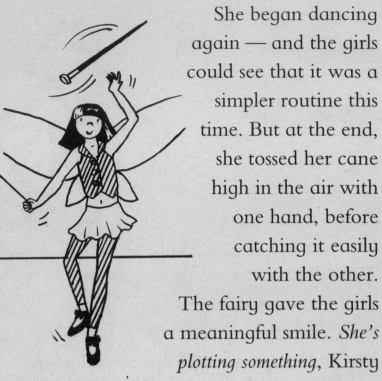

She began dancing
again — and the girls
could see that it was a
simpler routine this
time. But at the end,
she tossed her cane
high in the air with
one hand, before
catching it easily
with the other.
The fairy gave the girls
a meaningful smile. *She's
plotting something*, Kirsty
thought. *But what?*

The goblin began to dance the routine,
mimicking Tasha's steps exactly. The
ribbon on the cane fluttered as he tapped
like crazy.

Then, as the goblin neared the end of

the routine, Rachel and Kirsty both realized what Tasha was planning.

She's hoping the goblin will toss the cane into the air like she did, Kirsty thought. *And if he does, maybe Rachel or I can catch it!*

Kirsty held her breath as the goblin tapped his last steps.

"Now!" Tasha shouted to the girls, as the goblin flipped the cane into the air.

Happy Tapping

Kirsty darted forward with her arm outstretched and her gaze fixed on the falling cane. The goblin realized he'd been set up, and he jumped up to try and catch the cane, too.

But Kirsty was taller and she reached it first. "Got it!" she cheered, as her fingers closed around the cane.

She quickly untied the magic ribbon
and gave it to Tasha, who shrank it
down to its Fairyland size and reattached
it to her wand. A flurry of sparkles and
tiny top hats whirled around the wand as
it met the ribbon. The ribbon itself
shimmered with fairy magic.

"That's better!" Tasha beamed.
"Thanks, Kirsty!"

The goblin looked like
he couldn't quite
believe what had just
happened. "But . . ." he
stuttered. "But . . ."
He stomped his foot.
"You tricked me!" he yelled.

Rachel shook her head. "Tasha
won that ribbon fairly when she danced
better than you," she told him. "But you
wouldn't give it to her. So what choice
did we have?"

The goblin glared. "Thieves! Cheats!"
he yelled. "Tricksters!"

Tasha looked serious. "Jack Frost
shouldn't have taken the ribbons in the
first place," she reminded him. "He's
the thief, not us!"

"And you're a thief, too," Kirsty said to the goblin, "stealing someone else's tap shoes and cane like that!" The goblin stuck his tongue out. "Well, you're not getting the *shoes* back," he said, glancing down at them. "I'm keeping them to dance with." And as if to prove it, he started dancing. But without the ribbon's magical powers, he had no sense of rhythm or balance. Just seconds later, he tripped and landed on the floor.

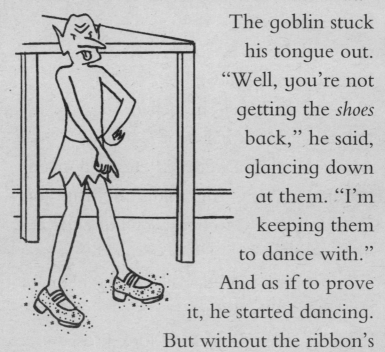

His face turned dark green with anger,

and he took off the shoes and threw them into a corner of the room.

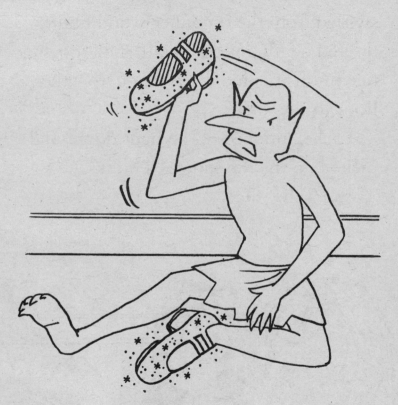

"Dumb shoes!" he muttered, then jumped to his feet and stomped off in disgust.

Tasha pointed her wand at the shoes. A stream of fairy dust and little top hats swirled from the tip of her wand and floated gently over to them. The shoes began tip-tapping their way across the floor to the girls!

Rachel laughed as she bent down and picked up the tap shoes. "Thanks, Tasha," she said.

"I should be thanking you two," Tasha replied. "You've both been wonderful, but now I must return to Fairyland with my ribbon! Good-bye, girls." And, blowing kisses to Rachel and Kirsty, Tasha disappeared in a shower of ruby red sparkles.

Rachel and Kirsty waved good-bye and then went to look for Ashleigh.

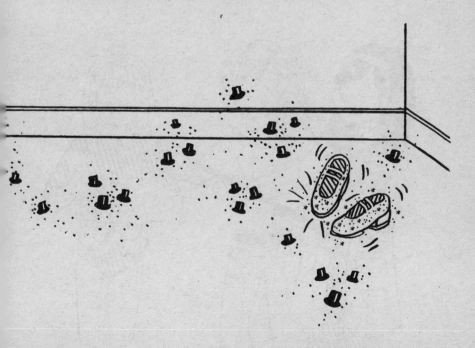

"Oh, thank you!" Ashleigh beamed when she saw her shoes and cane. "You saved the day! We're just about to start our show."

"You're welcome," Rachel said, smiling.

"We're looking forward to seeing you dance," Kirsty added.

Rachel and Kirsty watched as Ashleigh

ran over to join the rest of her dance class, ready for their performance. The teacher introduced the dance and turned on the music.

Rachel and Kirsty couldn't help feeling a tiny bit nervous as they watched — they'd seen so many dance performances go wrong lately! But this one went perfectly, and Ashleigh was a great dancer.

"And it's all because Tasha has her ribbon back again," Kirsty said happily.

"Yes," Rachel agreed with a grin. "I love helping the fairies!"

Tasha the Tap Dance Fairy has
her magic ribbon back. Now Rachel
and Kirsty must help

Jessica

the Jazz Fairy!

Join their next adventure in this special
sneak peek!

Jessica Makes an Entrance

"I'm sooo excited!" Kirsty Tate said happily, as she smoothed down the satin skirt of her long purple dress. "I've never been to a grown-up party before!"

"Me neither," Rachel Walker, Kirsty's best friend, agreed. Like Kirsty, she was dressed in a brand-new outfit, a floaty cream-colored dress with sequins around the hem and neckline. Along with Kirsty's parents, the girls were on their way to a party at the home of Alexander Willow, who was a friend of Mr. and Mrs. Tate's.

"It's not far now," Mr. Tate replied, steering the car down a dark, narrow country lane. "You're going to have a great time, girls. Alexander's a producer of Broadway musicals, and he always throws *fantastic* parties!"

"Yes, there's going to be a jazz band and lots of dancing!" added Mrs. Tate.

In the back of the car, Kirsty and Rachel exchanged an anxious glance.

"What kind of dancing will there be, Mom?" Kirsty asked. "Rachel and I don't really know what jazz dance is!"

Mrs. Tate nodded. "Jazz music is very

modern, and so is jazz dance," she
explained. "In fact, you've probably both
seen lots of jazz dancing in musicals."

"Oh, great!" Rachel exclaimed
happily, "I *love* that kind of dancing!"

Kirsty was staring out of the car
window, her eyes wide. "Rachel, look
at that pond with the mermaid fountain
in the middle."

Rachel gazed out of the window. "And
look at the house!" she added.

The manor house in front of them
looked very old. Its stone front was
beautiful with lots of windows and
a large wooden door that stood ajar.

A white tent had been set up in the
middle of the garden for the party. As the
girls walked in, they could see gold stars
sparkling from the ceiling of the tent.

Tables and chairs had been set up for the guests.

"Nobody's dancing yet, thank goodness!" Rachel whispered, noting the empty dance floor in the middle of the tent.

"Everyone's too busy eating and talking," Kirsty whispered back. "But there are lots of places for a goblin to hide!"

Rachel nodded. "We'll just have to keep looking," she said determinedly, scanning the party tent.

RAINBOW magic™
THE PET FAIRIES
When a pet finds a home, it's magical!

■SCHOLASTIC
www.scholastic.com
www.rainbowmagiconline.com

HiT entertainment

PET